RITA PHILLIPS MITCHELL was born in Belize but has lived
in the UK since the _____ She has worked as a primary teacher
as well as a teacher of _____ her picture books include
One for You, One for Me (Walker) *The Gotcha Smile* (Orchard).
She lives _____ x.

CAROLINE BINCH is the internationally acclaimed illustrator
of *Amazing Grace* and *Grace and Family (Boundless Grace)*
by Mary Hoffman, and *Down by the River* by Grace Hallworth.
She wrote and illustrated the picture books *Gregory Cool, Since Dad Left,*
New Born, Silver Shoes and *Cristy's Dream*, as well as one novel
for young readers about a traveller family, *Road Horse*.
Caroline lives in Cornwall.

For Leann and Brian – R.P.M.
For Enid and for Wilf – C.B.

JANETTA OTTER-BARRY BOOKS

First published in Great Britain and in the USA in 1992 by Victor Gollancz Ltd
This paperback edition first published in Great Britain in 2012 and in the USA in 2013
by Frances Lincoln Children's Books, 4 Torriano Mews,
Torriano Avenue, London, NW5 2RZ
www.franceslincoln.com

A catalogue record for this book is available from the British Library.

ISBN 978-1-84780-303-0

Illustrated with watercolours

Set in Berling Roman

Printed in Dongguan, Guangdong, China by Toppan Leefung in August, 2012

9 8 7 6 5 4 3 2 1

HUE
BOY

Rita Phillips Mitchell
Illustrated by Caroline Binch

FRANCES LINCOLN
CHILDREN'S BOOKS

Little Hue Boy was big news in his village. He was so small that all his friends towered over him.

Every morning Hue Boy's mother measured him.
    "Come, I must measure you before you go to school," she said. "Stand straight against the wall."
    It did not matter how straight Hue Boy stood, he remained the same size – very small. He didn't grow at all, at all.
    "Oh lawd!" cried Hue Boy's mother. "I wish your father was home. He would know what to do about this."
But Hue Boy knew his father was working on a ship, far away.

One day Mum said, "Hue Boy, if you want to grow tall
you must eat fresh vegetables and fruit every day."
"Like pumpkins?" said Hue Boy. "I like pumpkin soup."
"Pumpkins are good. But what about spinach, Hue Boy?"

"Yuck!" Hue Boy said. "I don't like spinach! I'd rather have fruit, like mangoes and melons."

"And pineapples and sapodillas, I suppose?" said Mum.

"Mm, yum, yum," said Hue Boy.

"How about sweet-sops, cashews and craboos?" his mother asked.

"Yes," said Hue Boy. "Delicious! And don't forget guavas or tamarinds, either."

"I won't, Hue Boy," said Mum.

Hue Boy was soon eating everything his mother gave him. The pumpkin soup was delicious, but he enjoyed eating fruit best.

Still, Hue Boy didn't grow one little bit. He didn't grow at all, at all.

On Hue Boy's birthday, his grandmother gave him
a special present.

"I've made you new clothes," she said. "You'll soon
grow into them."

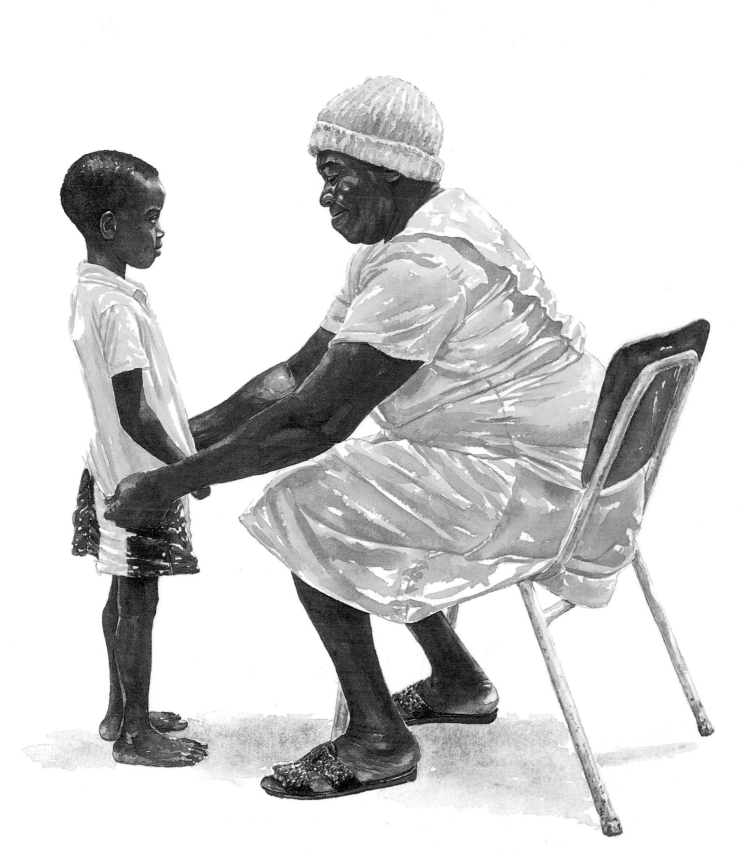

Hue Boy tried on the clothes. They felt a little loose.
"Lawdy! You look taller already," said Gran.

Then, one morning, their
neighbour Carlos said,
"I know, Hue Boy.
Some stretching exercises
will do the trick. Ten minutes
a day. That's all you need to do."

And so Hue Boy began
to do all sorts of exercises.
He stretched as much as he could.

Still, Hue Boy didn't grow
one little bit. He didn't grow at all, at all.

At school his classmates chanted:
  "Heels, heels, high-heeled shoes,
    Needed for the smallest boy in the school."
Hue Boy looked down.

But Miss Harper, the teacher, said, "Stuff and nonsense! Walk tall, Hue Boy. Hold your head up. That's all you need to do!"

Still Hue Boy didn't grow one little bit.

He didn't grow at all, at all.

Hue Boy's mother was worried. "Come, we must look for some help in the village," she said.

First they went to see the wisest man in the village. "Please, can you help Hue Boy to grow like other children?" said Mum.
  The wisest man of the village looked at Hue Boy from head to toe. Then from toe to head. "Well, Hue Boy," he said. "Where help is not needed, no help can be given."

Next day they visited Doctor Gamas. He examined Hue Boy thoroughly.

Then he said, "There is absolutely nothing wrong with you, Hue Boy. Some people are short and perfectly healthy, you know."

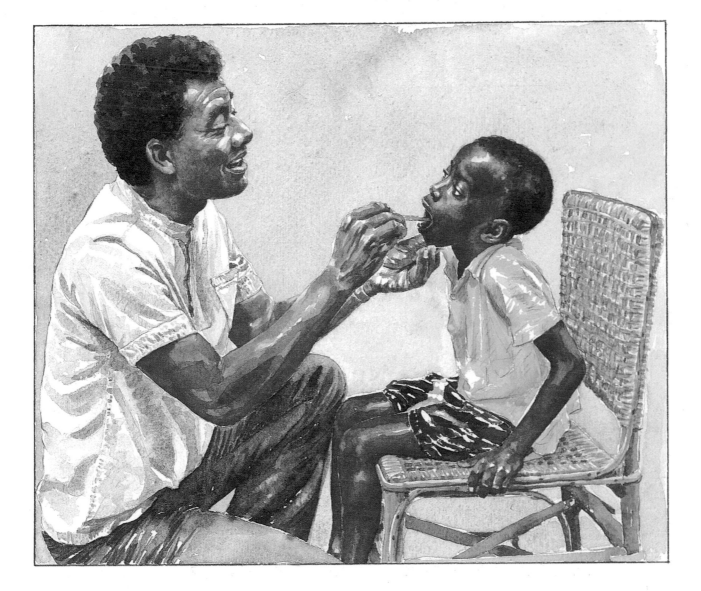

"Lawdy," cried Mum. "This problem seems to be bigger than this village!"

She thought carefully. "We ought to try Miss Frangipani, the Healer," she said. "Maybe she can help."

Hue Boy sighed. "I hope so."

"Miss Frangipani," said Mum.
"Please! Can you do something
for Hue Boy to make him grow?"
    "No problem," said Miss Frangipani.
"I alone hold the secret to growing!"

Miss Frangipani placed
a hand on Hue Boy's head
and said:

    "Ooooo! Ooooo!
    Grow-o, Grow-o.
    A touch of the hand;
    A wish of the mind,
    Comes the cure from far away.
    Ooooo! Ooooo!
    Grow-o, Grow-o.
    As you're meant to do."

Then Miss Frangipani gave
Hue Boy a bundle of herbs.
    "You must have your bath
with these," she told him.
"Mind you do it every night."

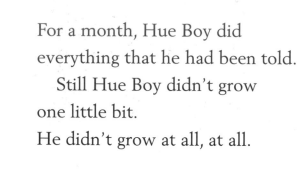

For a month, Hue Boy did
everything that he had been told.
Still Hue Boy didn't grow
one little bit.
He didn't grow at all, at all.

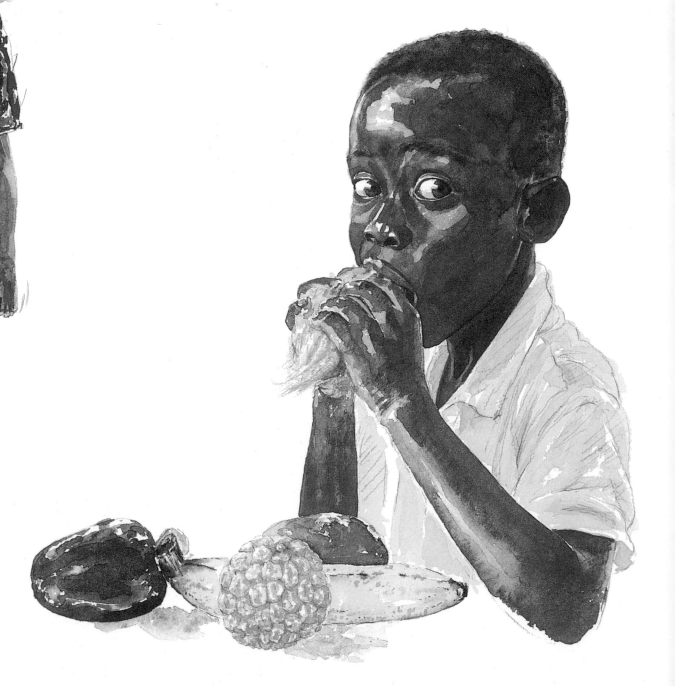

Sometimes Hue Boy liked to go
to the harbour. There he watched
the ships come and go and he could
forget about his size.

One day a beautiful big ship came in.
Man, that looks good! thought Hue Boy.
It's the biggest ship I ever saw!

Then Hue Boy saw a very tall man among
the passengers. The tall man walked
straight towards him.
    "Hello, Hue Boy," he said.
    "Dad!" said Hue Boy.

His father took Hue Boy's hand
and they walked away from
the harbour and into the village.

They walked past Miss Frangipani.
   They walked past Doctor Gamas
and the wisest man in the village.
   They walked past Miss Harper and Carlos.
   And they walked past Hue Boy's
friends from school.
   Then they met Gran and Mum.

And Hue Boy walked tall, with his head held high.
He was the happiest boy in the village.

And then something happened to Hue Boy. He began to grow.
At first he grew a little bit. Then he grew a little bit more.
Until the time came when his size didn't worry him any more.

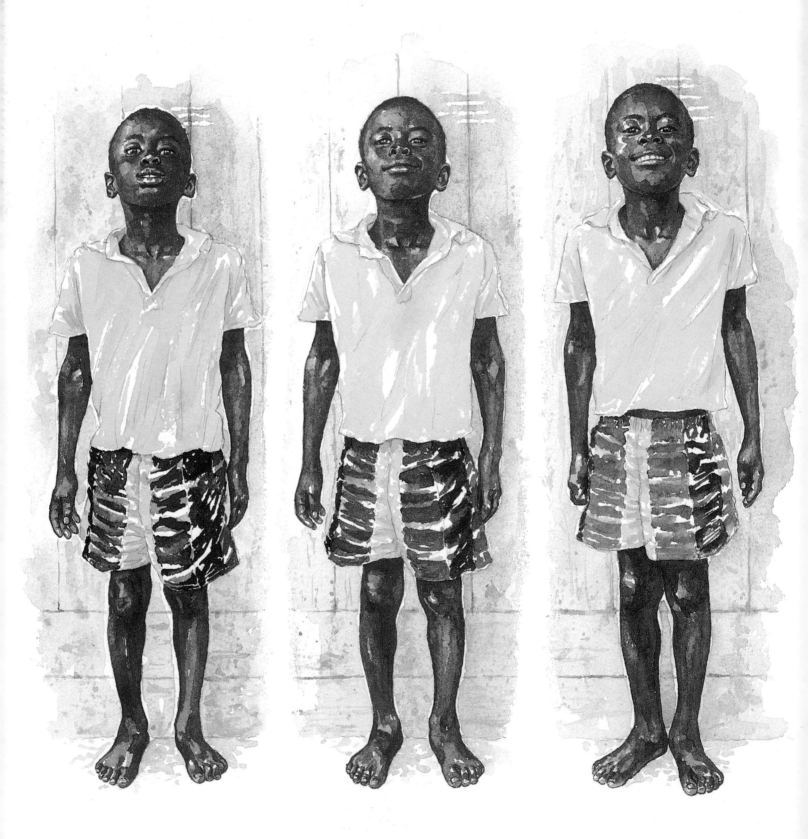

MORE BOOKS FROM FRANCES LINCOLN CHILDREN'S BOOKS

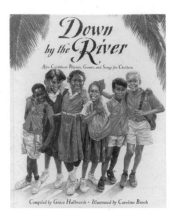

Down by the River
Grace Hallworth
Illustrated by Caroline Binch

A collection of African-Caribbean songs, games
and rhymes to play and say, with beautiful,
life-like watercolour illustrations.

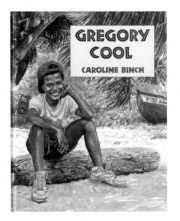

Gregory Cool
Written and illustrated by Caroline Binch

What happens when a cool city boy from London meets
his grandparents and cousins in Tobago for the first
time? This best-selling picture book is a moving story of
two cultures coming together, and new friendships.

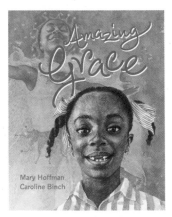

Amazing Grace
Mary Hoffman
Illustrated by Caroline Binch

The classic picture book, now in a new edition!

Read all about Grace, the girl who wants to be Peter Pan
in her school play. With a bit of help from Nana and
Ma, Grace finds out that if you put your mind to it,
you can be anything you want.